GOOD DRIVING, AMELIA BEDELIA

by **Herman Parish**
Pictures by **Lynn Sweat**

Greenwillow Books New York

Watercolors and a black pen were used for the full-color art.
The text type is Aldine 401.

Manufactured in China by South China Printing Company Ltd.
13 SCP 10 9

Library of Congress Cataloging-in-Publication Data
Parish, Herman
Good driving, Amelia Bedelia / by Herman Parish ;
pictures by Lynn Sweat.
p.   cm.
Summary: Amelia Bedelia's literalness
causes some problems when Mr. Rogers
takes her out to practice her driving.
ISBN 0-688-13358-4 (trade).
ISBN 0-688-13359-2 (lib. bdg.)
[1. Automobile driving—Fiction.
2. Humorous stories.]
I. Sweat, Lynn, ill.   II. Title.
PZ7.P2185Go   1995   [E]—dc20
94-4112   CIP   AC

FOR PEGGY PARISH,
THE REAL AMELIA BEDELIA
– H. P.

FOR KEVIN PHILLIP
AND AMANDA LYNN
–L. S.

Amelia Bedelia walked into the kitchen.

Mr. and Mrs. Rogers sang out,

"Happy Birthday, Amelia Bedelia!"

"Thank you," said Amelia Bedelia.

"Take the day off to celebrate,"

said Mrs. Rogers.

"I'll go and visit my cousin Alcolu,"
said Amelia Bedelia.

"Use our car," said Mr. Rogers.

"Oh, I have not driven in years,"
said Amelia Bedelia.

"Is your license still good?"
  asked Mrs. Rogers.
"It's great!" said Amelia Bedelia.
"See how nice my picture looks."

"Your license is fine," said Mr. Rogers.
"Let's see if your driving is as good
as your picture. Meet me at the car.
A short drive in the country
will do you good."

They backed out of the driveway
and away they went.
Amelia Bedelia drove very carefully.

"What a beautiful farm," said Mr. Rogers.

"Yes," said Amelia Bedelia.

"And what a nice bunch of cows."

"*Herd* of cows," said Mr. Rogers.

"Heard of cows?" asked Amelia Bedelia.

"Of course I have heard of cows."

"No," said Mr. Rogers. "I mean a cow *herd*."

"So what if a cow heard?" said Amelia Bedelia.

"I didn't say anything bad."

Some cows had wandered onto the road.

"Watch out!" said Mr. Rogers.

Amelia Bedelia stopped the car.

"Steer straight ahead," said Mr. Rogers.

"No," said Amelia Bedelia.

"The steer is behind us."

A cow with big horns looked into the car.
"Push on the horn," said Mr. Rogers.
Amelia Bedelia gently pushed
on the cow's horn.
MOOOOOOOOOOOOOOO!

Mr. Rogers pushed hard
on the car's horn.
HOOOOOOOOOOOOOOONK!
The cows ran back into the field.

Mr. Rogers took out a road map.

"I am looking for a crossroad," he said.

"It will have signs to tell us where to go."

"While you look, I'll go for a walk,"
  said Amelia Bedelia.

"Get some directions if you can,"
  said Mr. Rogers.

  Amelia Bedelia was back in five minutes.

"I did not find a cross road," she said.

"They were all very nice.

  But I got lots of directions.

  Would you like a 'North' or a 'South'?

  And I have a nice 'Southeast.' "

"*Now* we are lost," said Mr. Rogers.

"I have no idea where we are!"

"I know where we are," said Amelia Bedelia.

"We are right here."

Mr. Rogers looked back at his map.

They got back in the car.

"Should I look for another nice road?"
asked Amelia Bedelia.

"Don't you dare," said Mr. Rogers.

"Look for a fork in the road."

"I once looked for a needle in a haystack,"
said Amelia Bedelia.

"I never did find it."

Mr. Rogers pointed straight ahead.

"There is the fork," he said.

Amelia Bedelia looked very hard.

She saw that the road split into two roads.

"Which road is the fork in?"
  asked Amelia Bedelia.
"This road," said Mr. Rogers.
"I don't see any forks *or* spoons,"
  said Amelia Bedelia.
"Which way should I turn?"

"Turn left," said Mr. Rogers.

"Left?" asked Amelia Bedelia.

"Right," said Mr. Rogers.

"Okay, I will turn right,"
said Amelia Bedelia.

"Not *right*," said Mr. Rogers.

"Right is *not* right!"

"Well, right is not left,"
said Amelia Bedelia.

"That's right," said Mr. Rogers.

"Left *is* right! Right is *wrong*!"

"I am really mixed up,"
  said Amelia Bedelia.

"Right is wrong? Left is right?

Which way should I turn?"

"Bear left!" shouted Mr. Rogers.
So Amelia Bedelia made a sharp turn . . .
to the right.

"Amelia Bedelia!" shouted Mr. Rogers.

"Why did you turn right?"

"Because," said Amelia Bedelia,

"you warned me about the bear."

"*What* bear?" asked Mr. Rogers.

"You said there was a bear

  on the left," said Amelia Bedelia.

"There was no *bear*!" yelled Mr. Rogers.

"I said bear *left*."

"Oh," said Amelia Bedelia.

"If I'd known that the bear had left,

  I would not have turned right."

Mr. Rogers was about to blow up.

The tire beat him to it.

KAAAA-POWIE!

Thump! Thump! Thump!

"A flat tire!" said Mr. Rogers.
He got out to put on the spare.
Mr. Rogers opened the trunk.
He let out a big yell.

"What's wrong?" asked Amelia Bedelia.
"Did that bear come back?"

"Where is the spare tire?" said Mr. Rogers.
"And where is the jack?"
"I don't know where Jack went,"
    said Amelia Bedelia.
"Mrs. Rogers took everything
    out of the trunk yesterday.
    She said she had a lot to buy
    at the party store."

Mr. Rogers let out a sigh.

"This has been a long drive in the country,"
said Amelia Bedelia.

"The walk back to town
will be even longer," said Mr. Rogers.

"Stay here. I'll go and get help."

"Good luck," said Amelia Bedelia.

Mr. Rogers disappeared down the road.

Minutes later Amelia Bedelia

heard something coming.

It was not Mr. Rogers.

It was not even a car.

It was a tow truck.

"Need any help?" asked the driver.

"That depends," said Amelia Bedelia.

"Are you a Jack?"

"My name is John," he said.

"But you can call me Jack for short."

"I don't care how tall you are,"
 said Amelia Bedelia.

"If you are a Jack, you'll do."

Jack looked at the flat tire.

He pulled out a big nail.

"Here is your problem," said Jack.

"A nail?" said Amelia Bedelia.

"I thought I ran over a fork in the road."

Jack smiled. "Do you have a spare tire?"

"I'd like to give you one,"

said Amelia Bedelia.

"But we don't have enough good tires

for ourselves."

Jack smiled again.

"Would you like me to give you a tow?"

"I've got all the toes I need,"

said Amelia Bedelia.

"But could you pull our car back to town?"

"Good idea," said Jack.

He hooked up the car.

They drove down the road

and picked up Mr. Rogers.

Then they headed for home.

There was a big crowd
outside the Rogers house.
"Looks like a party," said Jack.
"How wonderful!" said Amelia Bedelia.

Mr. Rogers got out of the truck.

"Good heavens!" said Mrs. Rogers.

"You look run down!"

"Don't say that around Amelia Bedelia,"

said Mr. Rogers. "She might do it."

"Happy Birthday, Amelia Bedelia!"
said Cousin Alcolu.

"Hello, Cousin Alcolu," said Amelia Bedelia.

"Mr. Rogers was helping me practice
my driving so I could come to see you.
But we didn't get very far."

"That's okay," said Cousin Alcolu.

"I can drive. I can come to see you
anytime you want.
You will not have to drive at all."

Mr. Rogers shook his hand.
"Thank you, Cousin Alcolu.
It may be Amelia Bedelia's birthday,
but you just gave me the best present ever."

Amelia Bedelia cut giant slices
of birthday cake for everyone.
And nobody had to go out
to the road to find a fork.